Sophie Washington
Things You Didn't
Know About Sophie

Written by
Tonya Duncan Ellis

Books By
Tonya Duncan Ellis

Sophie Washington: Queen of the Bee

Sophie Washington: The Snitch

Sophie Washington:
Things You Didn't Know About Sophie

Sophie Washington: The Gamer

Sophie Washington: Hurricane

Table of Contents

Chapter 1

The Phone

He loves me. He loves me not.

I shrug my shoulders and tug the last petal off the cream-colored daisy, watching it drift to the floor. Then I scoot the mess under my bed with my feet. I have been playing this game every morning for the past week and come out losing more often than not.

"It's no use," I moan. "Toby will never like me!"

Toby Johnson joined our sixth-grade class this past fall, and it's as if I'm seeing things through 3D glasses. Mom hardly has to call me to come down for school in the morning, because I can't wait to get there. Our boring Texas history class is exciting now that Toby sits in the seat in front of me. Even P.E., which I've always hated, is fun, because Toby is in the class. He tells funny jokes, is good in sports, and talks to everyone, even the shy and quiet kids.

Toby is a good student, so the teachers like him, too. And, he has all kinds of neat stories to tell about his old school in Cleveland, Ohio, where his family moved from. Toby says that in Cleveland they have enough snow every winter to make snowmen as tall as he is. I've never seen snow, except once when we drove through some flurries on a road trip to New Mexico.

Things have been great since Toby got here, except he doesn't know I like him, and probably doesn't care. He's too busy making Goo Goo eyes at my best friend Chloe, the prettiest girl in the class. Not that I'm bad looking or anything, but next to her, I'm not so much. She's tall and has long, black, curly hair, and wears cute red bows and bracelets that make her look like a movie star, even in our school uniform. I, on the other hand, wear ponytails and need glasses to see the board.

No one knows how I feel about Toby. Not even Chloe. If anyone found out, I'd never come out of my room.

"Sophie, time for breakfast!" Mom calls.

I grab my backpack and rush out my bedroom door.

Bam! Me and my eight-year-old brother, Cole, collide.

"Move back, Creep!" he yells.

"Look where you're going, Blockhead," I counter.

"I *was* watching where I was going," he frowns. "You were just running through the house again like Mom and Dad told you not to."

I love my little brother, but he can be such a pain sometimes.

"Can you two please be nice to each other?" pleads Mom as we enter the kitchen, still grumbling.

"Cereal's for breakfast. I'm helping in Daddy's office this morning, so we need to leave early." Mom slides in her earrings and scrolls through her cell phone while we pour cornflakes into our bowls.

Our father is a dentist and has his own dental practice. Two or three days a week, Mom goes in to help him with accounting and checking in patients in his office in downtown Houston. Since we attend Xavier Academy, a private school that doesn't have a school bus, she drives us to school every morning.

Mom's been working with our father most days recently because the city had heavy rains earlier this spring. A couple of weeks ago, his office flooded. It rained for 40 days and 40 nights, like Noah's ark. Dad had to see patients in a building across the street while repairs were being made. A lot of his medical equipment was ruined. Dad left his cell phone there and it got water damage, and still needs to be replaced. I don't know how he can stand being without it. He's been using an old flip phone until he has time to buy a new one.

I didn't go in the office when it was filled with water, but Mom told me it was up to her knees.

The suburb we live in has good drains, thank goodness, so our neighborhood didn't flood. But, water rose up to the waists of some statues of children playing near a gas station a few blocks down from our house, and someone put life jackets on them as a joke.

My friend Mariama's house did flood, and her family had to actually float down their street in kayaks. Lucky for them, they didn't see any alligators swimming around, because, believe it or not, there are some alligators in the waterways in our area. My dad jokes that they could film our suburb on the *Animal Planet* channel.

"Your birthday is coming up in a couple of weeks, Sophie," says my father, joining the rest of us in the kitchen. "What gift would you like this year?"

I grin. I can't believe that I'll soon be 11 years old. Seems like just yesterday I was turning double digits. "Since you asked, there is something very special I would like for my birthday," I say, smiling shyly.

"I hope it's not a sleepover like you had last year," says Cole. "I don't want to have to leave the house just because a lot of icky girls are here."

"If I get what I want, I can talk to my friends without you even seeing them," I tell my brother.

"I think I know where this conversation is going, and I don't know if I like it," says Mom. "You know how I feel about preteens having cell phones."

"But I'm the only one of my friends without one!" I whine. "It's not fair."

"Use the landline," Mom suggests.

"The home phone doesn't have a contact list, or a way for Sophie to remember her friends' phone numbers like a cell phone does," says Cole, coming to my rescue.

I've got to give it to the kid; he realizes that any win for me will be a win for him, since he's spoiled rotten and always gets to do everything way earlier than I ever did.

"It might be something to consider, Honey," says Dad, to my surprise. He turns to my mother. "The kids have been staying after school more often with you helping out so much at the office. That would be a way for us to contact them more easily if we have any delays."

"You're the best Dad ever!" I run to give him a hug.

"This isn't settled yet," Mom says, grabbing her car keys from her purse. "Your Dad and I will discuss this later. Finish up your breakfast and let's get ready to go."

Daddy gives me a wink as we move to the garage. I wonder what color phone case I will get?

Chapter 2

Dodgeball

"Hey girl!" My good friends Chloe and Mariama smile and head my way as I close my locker to go to first period. We've been BFFs since fifth grade. Mariama's family is from Nigeria, and last year for our school's twin day, we dressed up as triplets, and her mom made all three of us colorful African dresses to wear. She used to be kind of shy, but she has come out of her shell.

I spy Toby across the hallway at his locker and my heart flutters.

He's wearing cute, red Nike sneakers that match his uniform polo shirt. He turns our way and grins, showing his dimples.

"Oh no, Toby is coming over here," says Chloe, stashing her cell phone in her book bag.

"What's wrong with that?" I ask.

"He's so annoying," she says. "Always bragging about how he used to play in the snow in

Cleveland, and how great their basketball team is because they have LeBron."

"He's probably just trying to get your attention," says Mariama.

"Well, he is, in the worst way."

Toby walks to our lockers and says hello to Chloe, basically ignoring me and Mariama. Chloe mumbles something about needing to get to class and we make our way down the hall.

It's no fair. Some people have all the luck. The only boys who pay attention to me are my brother, my dad, and my friend Nathan Jones from school, and they don't count. Dad loves me no matter what I do, and Cole just wants to get me in trouble. I actually do like Nathan. Even though I beat him in the school spelling bee last year, he helped me and my friends stand up to a bully named Lanie, who was terrorizing everyone in our class.

The day moves on as usual, and soon it's time for P.E., my least favorite class. That's something else all my friends don't know about me. I hate team sports. I sit through Cole's basketball games because my parents make me, but I usually bring a book to read. I like running, but I'm smaller than a lot of the other kids, and I'm not as strong or fast. I'm always one of the last ones picked for teams. That's fine with me, because I usually try to do as little as possible. Mom says I will hit a growth spurt and things will change. So far, it hasn't happened.

The only problem is, Toby loves sports. And Chloe, the tallest girl in class, is also one of the best girl athletes. I think that's one of the reasons he notices her.

Today, I'm going to change all that. When Mr. Greeley, the P.E. coach, announces that we're playing dodgeball, I step to the front of the group rather than hiding behind all the other kids, as usual.

"What are those socks you have on, Sophie?" asks Chloe, looking curiously at my ankles.

"Oh, just my new LeBron's," I say, raising my voice so the boys standing nearby can hear me. I actually fished them out of Cole's hamper this morning, but what they don't know won't hurt them.

"You like basketball socks?" asks Nathan Jones quizzically.

"Oooh, look at those Lebron's, man," says Josiah Joseph. "I've been begging my mom to buy them for me for the past month."

"Those are smooth," agrees Toby, shaking his head in appreciation.

I turn my back to Nathan and move closer to the other boys. "He's my favorite player," I lie.

Chloe raises her eyebrow.

Toby and Josiah are team captains, and to everyone's surprise, the first person Toby picks is me. The boys go back and forth choosing, and Nathan, who's the shortest boy in the class, is the last one left, so he goes on Josiah's team.

"Looks like I got all the best players," taunts Toby.

"We'll see about that," Nathan replies.

We line up on opposite sides of the gym. Chloe and Mariama are on Josiah's team. Coach flips a coin and our team gets the ball first. Toby hurls it so the ball bounces off Mariama's ankle.

"Boo yah!" he yells.

Three people quickly get out on our team and I high-tail it to the back corner of the gym. Everyone is scrambling around, laughing and screaming.

Nathan somehow gets the ball and throws it at Toby's head with all his might.

"Missed me, Shrimp!" Toby laughs, smoothly gliding out of the way.

But before he moves to safety, Chloe nabs the ball and beans him on the chest. "You're out!"

He shakes he head, laughing, and moves to the side of the gym.

"The ball just rolled over near you, Sophie," shouts Toby. "Get it!"

I spot the red rubber ball seconds before Chloe, and realize we are the last two players left. All the kids cheer as I reach down to grab the ball. Chloe turns to run; too late.

I heave the ball and it hits her behind, and bounces across the gym. Bull's eye!

Toby runs to give me a high five. Our team won!

Chapter 3

Texas History

"You didn't have to hit me so hard," says Chloe, rubbing her backside in the locker room. "I will probably have a bruise."

"I'm sorry, Chloe," I say. "I didn't realize how hard I was throwing the ball." Really, I'm not sorry. For the first time in forever, I beat "Ms. It" and it feels good.

"And since when do you like LeBron? Did you really buy those socks?"

"I borrowed them from Cole," I admit, stuffing them in my backpack. "But I do think LeBron is cool."

My two friends look at me like I'm a Martian. We all know I care as much about LeBron James as I do Texas history. There's no way I will admit it, though. I'm finally getting Toby's attention.

"Good game, Sophie," says Mariama, gathering up her backpack. "Guess we'll see you after eighth period."

"OK, see you."

I walk out of the locker room and head to my Texas history class. Before Toby came on the scene, this was where I did most of my daydreaming. But he actually seems to like the class and asks lots of questions, which has encouraged me to pay attention.

Once the bell rings and everyone settles in their seats, Mrs. Laurel, our teacher, makes an announcement.

"I have some exciting news to share with you students! This morning I got approval for our Texas history field trip to Austin. We will drive to our state's capital next Monday to see some of the historic sites we've been studying, up close and personal. Please have your parents sign these permission slips I'm passing out, this evening if you're going, and return them to class tomorrow."

"Wow, that should be fun!" Toby high-fives his friend Luke in the next row over.

I'm pretty happy myself. Not only will we get to miss a day of school, but I'll also be able to spend most of the day with Toby without Chloe around. She has dyslexia and takes a special session of social studies that gives her more time for her work. Dyslexia is a learning disability that makes it harder for her to read than other kids. Up until this year, she's taken all her classes with the rest of us, but in sixth grade they have a special session for students with learning disabilities. I miss not seeing Chloe as much during the day, but this time I'm not complaining that things have changed.

"Hey Toby, did you study Ohio history when you lived in Cleveland?" I ask.

"Nah, we just had regular social studies," he answers. "It wasn't as interesting as Texas history. I like learning about all the cowboys from back in the day."

"But you all have snow in Ohio, which is pretty neat," I say.

"Yeah, that is something I miss," he replies.

Toby tells me that his family moved to Houston because his mother got a job as an engineer at an oil company. He says he has an eight-year-old brother named Michael, and a turtle named Leonardo.

I tell him about my pet fish, Goldy. "I wanted to get a dog, but my mom has allergies," I explain.

Once class is over, Toby walks with me to my locker.

"Catch you later," he says as Chloe and Mariama join us. "How you doing, Chloe? I really like that bow."

"Thank you," she says while Toby gives her the biggest grin I've ever seen.

"Ick, I can't stand that creep!" she exclaims after he walks off.

"Why don't you like him?" asks Mariama.

"He's just goofy, that's all," responds Chloe.

I change the subject.

"Our Texas history class is taking a trip to Austin next week."

"Yeah, we're going, too," says Mariama. "I think they are taking the entire grade."

"I'll be glad to miss a day from school," says Chloe. "I wonder what we'll have for lunch?"

My heart sank. I thought I was going to have Toby all to myself. Now I'll have to figure out how to get his attention again.

Chapter 4

Up on the Housetop

When we pull up to our driveway after school, we have an unwelcome surprise.

Two black buzzards perch on our roof like they own the place.

"Not again!" Mom shrieks.

She toots the horn, and instead of flying off, they just stare. Then the largest one spreads its wings three feet wide, as if to say, "Welcome home."

"Those things are just disgusting," Mom cries. "I don't know why they keep coming back here."

For the past two weeks we've been trying to get rid of the buzzards. The birds stand as tall as Cole was when he was three years old, and have dark-colored feathers, red heads and white beaks. At least six or seven have been roosting on our roof, leaving feathers and their bird poop behind.

Buzzards are scavengers, meaning they eat other dead animals, so Dad had a company come and clean out the gutters on our house to make sure there were no dead squirrels or mice there. They went away for a day or two, but now they are back.

When they first came, Mom called the wildlife society to see if there was anything we could do, but they said the buzzards have no natural predators or other animals that eat them that they are afraid of. It's against the law to shoot or harm them, because they are an endangered species.

"Get out of here!" she yells.

We look at her like she's crazy.

"You kids don't understand," she says, shaking her fists at the roof. "Those nasty birds may carry all sorts of diseases."

"What's that white stuff?" asks Cole, pointing to the bird poop on the rooftop. "Is it snow?"

"That does it!" Mom exclaims.

"Cole, go get that bouncy ball from your toy box," she says, opening the back door.

"What are you going to use it for?" he asks.

"You'll see."

When Cole gets back, Mom takes his ball and flings it on the roof.

"Awwwk," squawk two of the buzzards, flying away.

"That's right, get out of here you nasty things!" Mom exclaims.

I run in and find a rubber ball from a jacks set I have, and throw it up to the birds. It narrowly misses hitting one of the buzzards in the head. The bird looks at me indignantly, then joins his friends in the sky.

"Look over there!" Cole points to the backyard.

Two more buzzards fight over a dead squirrel between their beaks.

"Maybe that's why they are here," says Mom.

She grabs the water hose and sprays it on them, and they soar off with the carcass.

"I hope that will be the last of them," says Mom. "Those things scare me to death. They are nearly as big as your brother."

That night at dinner, we tell Dad about our scavenger adventure.

"I kind of like buzzards," he says. "They are nature's way of cleaning up the environment. Without them, we would have dead squirrels, armadillos and other roadkill lying around."

"Well, to me they are just plain gross," says Mom. "I can't wait until we get another good rain to clean our roof off."

"Then the snow will wash away," Cole protests.

"That's not snow, silly," I say, laughing at my brother, "it's bird poop!"

"Ewww!" he says, scrunching up his nose.

"Watch your language, young lady," scolds Mom. "We are at the dinner table."

"Buzzard droppings probably aren't something Santa would want to land his sleigh on this Christmas," jokes Dad. "Pass me the mashed potatoes."

"Awwwk!" I shriek.

Chapter 5

Keep Austin Weird

"All aboard!" Mrs. Laurel and another sixth-grade social studies teacher, Mr. Clancey, stand near the charter bus door with clipboards, checking off names on the list of children for our Texas history trip to Austin.

"Let's sit near the back," Chloe whispers to me and Mariama.

I see Toby and his friends making their way down the aisle toward the back of the bus, and happily agree.

Nathan moves his leg in a gesture for me to join him when I pass his seat, but I keep moving.

The bus trip to Austin will take two and a half hours. It should be fun, but may get kind of boring for me, because all my friends have their cell phones to listen to music and play games with, and I have nothing. Even Mariama has a phone, and she's from another country.

Mom says she and Dad are still thinking about letting me have one. My birthday is less than two weeks from now, so I hope they make their decision soon.

Mariama and I settle into a seat together and Chloe gets in a seat beside us where she can stretch out her long legs. I'm glad I'm near the window so I can check out the countryside as we go by. My parents have been to Austin a few times on business trips, but have never taken me and Cole with them.

A large field of pretty blue wildflowers shimmers like ocean waves as we drive by.

"Those are bluebonnets," says Mrs. Laurel, "our state flower."

I've seen patches of bluebonnets along the road in Houston, but these stretch on as far as the eye can see.

"I wish we could get out and take some pictures," Mariama says admiringly.

After about an hour of driving, we stop at a *Buc-ee's* rest stop to eat lunch. Though it's not one of the landmarks we study in Texas history, I think it should be. *Buc-ee's* is a huge store and gas station that has a neat sign of a beaver with a red baseball cap on his head out front. It has big clean restrooms, and lots of good food and candy to buy. Cole used to have a *Buc-ee's* t-shirt that he wore all the time before it got too small.

We get out of the bus and head to picnic tables in a grassy area. Mr. Clancey passes out sack lunches and we open them up to see what's inside. Just what I don't want: frozen turkey sandwiches, carrot sticks, pretzels and a water bottle. Lucky for me, Mom gave me extra cash to get souvenirs and snacks if I want.

"You may go inside in groups of three to make purchases," Mrs. Laurel tells us. "We will be doing a roll call and getting back onto the bus in exactly thirty minutes."

"Let's get some snacks," I suggest to Chloe and Mariama.

We make our way inside the store, and I buy some fudge and beef jerky. We go back outside to finish up eating and see Toby and some other kids running around in a field. Nathan stumbles and Toby helps him up.

"See, he's not so bad, is he?" I say.

"Hmmmph!" Chloe replies. "Toby's the one who tripped him."

Soon, it's time to head back to the bus for the second half of our trip.

The phones keep most of the kids quiet; the parents and the chaperones are doing most of the talking.

It doesn't look like I will have a chance to hang out with Toby like I'd hoped, because for most of the drive he has been laughing at YouTube videos with his friends.

As we get closer to Austin's capital, Toby looks up from his device. "You forget your phone, Sophie?"

"No," I say, "it's a new iPhone and my parents didn't want me to risk losing it on the trip."

"You got an iPhone?" asks Chloe, eyes wide. "How come you haven't called me yet?"

"I haven't set it up," I lie again. "I wanted to keep it a secret to surprise you all."

"That's cool," exclaims Mariama. "Call us on it when you get home and we can add you to our group chat."

I'm surprised.

"Group chat? What's that?"

"It's a text where we all send messages to each other at the same time about school and stuff," Toby explains.

Why would Chloe and Mariama want to be in a group chat with Toby when Chloe says she doesn't even like him? And, what am I going to say if I don't get a phone?

Mrs. Laurel interrupts my thoughts. "Look students! There is our state's capital."

The Texas state capital building is larger and different than I'd imagined. I had pictured it being the color of the White House in Washington, DC, but it is an amber tint. Burnt orange street signs with Texas Longhorn symbols, the mascot of the University of Texas, are all over the place. Even some of the homeless people we see are wearing t-shirts with the UT logo on them.

"They have a lot of school spirit here, don't they?" jokes Toby, pointing out a Longhorn statue in front of a McDonald's restaurant.

Unlike Houston, which is very flat, Austin winds up and down with huge hills. Two college-age girls wearing shirts that say "Keep Austin Weird," make their way up the street.

"What does that mean?" I ask Mrs. Laurel.

"Austin is known for its art, culture and music," she says. "They want the city to stay unique."

My friends pull out their devices to snap photos of the sights and sounds of Austin, and I remember that I need to convince my parents to get me a cell phone, ASAP.

Chapter 6

Lady Bird Lake

After a visit to the state capital, we tour the Bullock Texas State History Museum. The museum has neat exhibits that tell the story of how Texas was settled and became a part of the United States. It has cool artifacts that have been saved from our state's history, like old coins, clothes, guns and famous documents, and also includes a huge IMAX theater that runs new movies.

On the way out, our class takes a picture in front of the gigantic star in front of the museum.

"The first flag of the Republic of Texas had one gold star on it," Mr. Clancey says. "That's why Texas is known as the Lone Star State."

When the tours are over, we head to Lady Bird Lake in Zilker Park. It's in the middle of the downtown area, so you can see city buildings on either side. People are riding up and down the lake in canoes, kayaks and paddleboards.

"Lady Bird Lake is a reservoir, or storage space for fluids," explains Mrs. Laurel. "Who knows where the water in the lake comes from?"

Toby and Nathan both raise their hands, but she gestures to Toby. "Is it the Colorado River?" he answers.

"Exactly," she beams. "I see someone has been studying his Texas history. It was created in 1960, and named after former First Lady, Lady Bird Johnson in the 1970s, because she started a project to keep the lake beautiful. Good job, Toby."

Nathan frowns.

"Since we have a smaller group, and you have been so well-behaved today, we have a special treat," Mrs. Laurel adds. "Nathan's father, Mr. Jones, has offered to purchase kayak rides for all who are interested."

"Yay!" shout the students.

"We will have an hour ride, and then stop for a nice dinner on our way back to school."

"That's so cool!" grins Chloe. "I've always wanted to ride in a kayak."

I don't feel too happy. I'm a pretty good swimmer, but for as long as I can remember, I've been jittery around boats. Mom says I fell off a water raft one time in the neighborhood pool when I was a toddler, and that's why I'm scared.

I'm just getting ready to move back and sit this one out when Toby walks toward me and my friends.

"Are you all going to ride in a boat? Maybe we can go together."

"Everyone, let's line up for instructions," says Mrs. Laurel. "If you want to ride in a kayak, raise your hand."

Twenty of the 30 kids present, including me, put our hands in the air.

"Those who want to sit out can stay here with me. You will kayak in groups of two to that bridge in the distance, and then return here. All boaters must wear life jackets; no exceptions. We will have one girl and one boy in each kayak. The person sitting in back will steer the kayak, and the person in the front helps move it along."

The man working at the kayak booth helps us put on our lifejackets. I choose a red one with black straps. Next, he demonstrates how to steer the oars.

"Make sure not to wiggle around too much or you might tip over," he warns.

What have I gotten myself into?

I look around for Toby and see him rushing into a kayak with Chloe.

That's just great.

Mariama is sitting with Mrs. Laurel, like someone with good sense.

"I rode in kayaks enough after our house flooded, and I never want to get in one again," she explains.

"Will you ride with me, Sophie?" Nathan Jones asks.

He's the last person I want to see. If it weren't for his Big Shot father, I wouldn't be in this mess in the first place. Nathan and I used to be enemies when we competed against each other in the fifth grade spelling bee, but after he helped me fight off our class bully, Lanie Mitchell, last year, we've become pretty good friends.

"Sure," I say with a forced smile.

Chloe is actually grinning from ear to ear, which I cannot believe. She snaps on a fluorescent yellow life jacket and moves with Toby to a green boat.

Nathan and I carefully get into our blue kayak, and then the guide pushes us out into the water.

"Since you're in the back, you need to steer," Nathan instructs.

I sit still, wide-eyed.

"It's easy," he reassures me. "Just push on the side opposite the one we want to move in."

I push my oar in the water and we start moving in closer to the rest of our class.

"Have you done this before?" I ask Nathan.

"Yeah, we've come to Austin a few times when my dad needed to buy supplies for Fun Plex," he answers. "He let us rent the boats as a break."

Fun Plex is an entertainment center that Nathan's family owns. They have bumper cars, video games and food. I've been to more birthday parties there than I can count, and I never get tired of going, but I'm sure it's not Nathan's favorite place, since his Dad is kind of strict and has him there working nearly every weekend.

While we're talking, I get out of rhythm with my steering. We move toward a large bush on the riverbank.

"Ahhh! We're going the wrong way!" I shriek. "What do I do?"

Three turtles the size of fat throw pillows sun themselves on a rock in front of us. The boat is moving in the path of the widest one.

"Row on the other side of the kayak," Nathans warns. "Quick!"

An ivory swan glides past us and honks a warning. I swipe my oar through the water quickly, and we narrowly miss ramming into turtle rock, but instead hit the prickly bush.

"Keep steering!" Nathan yells, swiping the brambles out of his path.

Sweat runs down my forehead while I look to see where the rest of the class is floating. The nine other boats are about a football field away from us, and are getting ready to turn around at the bridge.

For the next half hour we slowly spin in circles as I try to gain control of the kayak.

"If we can't get straight, we may have to jump out and switch places so I can steer," Nathan suggests.

Finally, I turn us in the direction of the riverbank before anyone sees us.

Nathan wipes perspiration off his glasses on his t-shirt. "Just keep your oar to the side and I'll take over."

Toby and Chloe glide next to us and he shows his dimples. "How's it going, Sophie?"

"Oh, just great!" I pipe up, and put on a bright smile.

Nathan looks at me quizzically.

"This has been the best field trip ever!" Chloe enthuses.

My arms feel like rubber by the time we make our way back to the riverbank. I'm so happy to touch the ground I want to kiss it. I pretend to sleep on the drive to the restaurant for dinner, while my classmates chatter about all the fun they had on the kayaks. I will be happy when this day is over.

Chapter 7

Food Fight

The bus winds around the park until we stop at a parking lot near a brightly colored restaurant. *Chuy's Fine Tex Mex* reads the orange, blue and yellow sign. I've heard of this restaurant in Houston, but I guess it got its start in Austin.

We pile out of the bus and head inside for dinner. My stomach is rumbling, because I didn't eat much but fudge for lunch.

"Welcome! Is this the group from Xavier Academy?" asks the host who comes to greet us. He looks not much older than a high schooler, but has a long beard and mustache, and tattoos on his arms.

"Yes, that's us," Mrs. Laurel smiles.

The restaurant has a lively atmosphere with music playing. It feels kind of like a 1950's style diner that I've seen in old movies with my parents. The walls are salmon colored, and the floor is covered with blue, yellow, red and white tiles. There are pictures of the old singer Elvis Presley, and real, old-time 45 records on the wall.

The host takes us to a table in the back of the restaurant that has orangey walls with pictures of Cadillac cars on them, and actual hubcaps on the ceiling.

"I hope none of those fall and hit us on the head," laughs Chloe.

I feel much better once I start eating chips and salsa, and place my order for tacos, rice and beans. Even though the kayak ride was scary, it was kind of exciting when I think back on it.

"What did you order, Sophie?" asks Toby, moving to the table with me, Chloe, Mariama and Josiah.

"Tacos," I say.

"Me too," he answers. "They say this place has the best Tex-Mex in Austin."

"I've eaten here a few times when we've come down to Austin, and it is pretty good," Nathan adds, and pulls a chair over to our table.

"I don't think there is enough room here," says Toby.

"Yes there is," Nathan answers. "Mrs. Laurel says we should have at least five to a table. I can just sit here on the edge."

As he slides his way in, Nathan spills some of his lemonade on Toby's lap.

"Great, look what you did now!" Toby frowns.

"Well, you should have moved over and given me room," Nathan responds, shoving him.

Toby shoves Nathan back. Then Nathan grabs a handful of chips and throws it at him.

"Stop it!" yells Mariama.

Nathan picks up the bowl of salsa, ready to dump it on Toby's head.

"Looks like you kids had a little too much of the Texas heat today," says a female server, grabbing the bowl from Nathan before any damage is done. "Why don't I add a table here so that you can cool off before your food is ready?"

She pulls a smaller square table from the corner of the room and adds it to ours. Nathan, Mariama and I scoot to the end to wait for our food.

That was a close one. If Mrs. Laurel or Mr. Clancey had seen what was going on, we'd all be in trouble.

"Why did you do that, Nathan?" I ask. "Toby didn't do anything to you."

"Yeah, it figures you would take that jerk's side, as usual," he says. "You think he's so great, but he's not."

"You're just jealous, Nathan Jones!" I fume.

We don't say much for the rest of dinner, though the food is some of the best Tex-Mex I've ever had.

Nathan pushes by Toby without a word when we load back on the bus. I still don't understand why he is so mad. Boys!

Chapter 8

Plan B

I was sleepy the next day after school. We got home from the field trip after 11:00 p.m., and I didn't rest well for worrying about how I was going to persuade my parents to buy me not just a cell phone, but the latest iPhone. Thankfully, my friends didn't ask about it. They were too busy talking about all the fun we had, and groaning about the extra work our teachers were giving us to make up for the school we missed during our trip to Austin. But, I know that won't last long. I've got to act fast.

Everyone also seemed to have forgotten about Nathan and Toby's food fight. The boys didn't talk to each other all day long, but at least they also didn't brawl.

I finish up my homework, and then make a peanut butter sandwich and a glass of milk for a snack. I grab the family laptop before Cole gets it to sneak and play his favorite video games, as he does most days after school. When my mother asks, he claims he's on a website called Quizlet that helps him study, but I know better.

"What'cha looking at, Sophie?" Cole leans over my shoulder as I scroll through Apple.com.

"Mind your own business, Twerp."

"Why are you always so mean to me?" he whines. "I just want to talk."

"Yeah right. What do you want, Cole?"

"Nothing." He makes a grab for the computer.

"Get off, Cole! I was here first."

Cole tries to arm-wrestle me out of the way, but I'm too quick for him. I snatch the laptop and slide to a loveseat across the room.

"What is all that noise going on in there?" Mom yells from her bedroom. "If I hear anymore ruckus, both of you are doing dish duty for the rest of the week!"

We quiet down, and Cole decides to sneak and play his Nintendo DS as an alternative, so I go back to the laptop in peace.

I have to blink when I see how much an iPhone costs. *Eight hundred dollars! There's no way my parents will buy me that for my birthday.*

"What am I going to do?" I say out loud.

"About what?" asks Cole, continuing to play on his DS. "Is it about getting a new phone?"

"Yeah, but there's nothing I can do about it," I say dejectedly. "All my friends are going to find out that I'm a phony."

"I know where you can get an iPhone for free," he offers.

"They don't give those phones away free anywhere," I say.

"I saw a new iPhone in Dad's office when we went after school yesterday while you were on the field trip," he replies.

"Are you sure?" I ask.

He nods his head. "I wanted to open it to play with, but Mom said no."

It must be the phone Dad bought to replace the one that got ruined in the flood!

"I owe you one, Twerp!" I say, giving him a quick hug that he shrugs off.

I hand him the laptop. "I'm through with my work. It's all yours."

"Thanks!" he says in surprise.

I skip off happily to the stairs and head to my room. It's time to organize Plan B.

Chapter 9

Game Night

Now that I know my father has an extra cell phone in his office, the solution to my problem is simple. I have to find a way to get Mom to take me there this weekend, nab the phone out of the drawer, and bring it to school to show my friends. Maybe my parents will buy me some kind of cell phone for my birthday in the meantime, and I can tell everyone I had to exchange the iPhone when I return Dad's.

Skipping down to eat, I feel more relaxed than I have in days. *Everything is going to work out.*

Dinner is one of my favorites: taco salad with a spread of ground beef, fajita chicken, lettuce, tomatoes, peppers, onions, black olives, black beans, nacho chips and cheddar cheese. Mom puts all the fixings in separate dishes on the counter so we can all make our own.

"I want to see some vegetables on your plate, young man," she fusses at Cole, who fills his plate with meat and cheese, as usual. "You need to at least eat some lettuce."

"Yes Ma'am," he answers, picking at two cherry tomatoes.

Afterwards, we clean the dishes and gather for Family Game Night.

Since my dad works late many evenings at his dental office, Mom decided we should have a family game night at least twice a month. Instead of watching television, we spend about an hour playing a board game. Sometimes Cole gets on my nerves when he starts cheating, but mostly it's pretty fun.

"What does everyone want to play tonight?" asks Dad.

"How about Scrabble?" suggests Mom.

"That's too hard for me. I never win," Cole complains. "I want to play Battleship."

"Only two people can play that game, Son," Dad replies.

"I know, let's play Monopoly!" I say.

"OK, but if the game goes on for more than an hour, we will have to put it up for next time," says Mom. "You guys have school in the morning."

We pick our men while Mom sets up the board. I choose the shoe, Dad is the top hat, Cole gets the battleship, and Mom picks the car. The game starts, and after the dice roll, Cole gets to go first and I am last.

"Being last means everyone else will get all the property before my turn," I pout.

"Be patient, Sophie," soothes Mom. "You never know what will happen."

I am right.

By the time my turn comes, Reading Railroad, St. Charles Place and Virginia Avenue are gone. I keep landing on Chance and Community Chest, and owing money.

I see Cole slipping money out of the bank and into his pile.

"Cheater!" I shout. "You can't get money out of the bank until you pass Go."

Cole gives a sheepish grin and returns the bills.

Mom and Dad buy Kentucky Avenue, B & O Railroad and Marvin Gardens, and I still have nothing.

Forty-five minutes into the game, and I am ready to call it quits.

"It's no use playing anymore." I throw down the two bills I have left after landing on Cole's Boardwalk hotel and paying him off. "There's no way I will win."

"It's not always about winning, Sophie," says Dad. "It's about enjoying spending time together. I'm not doing as well as your mother or brother, but do you see me complaining? Continuing until you finish the game may teach you some tips on how to do better next time."

I roll again and land on Baltic Avenue. Usually I'm happy to move to this cheap property, because the rents you owe are low, but Cole has two hotels on it, so I have to pay up.

"I'm rich!" he grins, gathering up his huge stack of bills.

"You always have to brag when you win!" I say, then jiggle the game board so that all the pieces move out of place.

"Sophie Washington!" Mom exclaims.

"She's just a sore loser," says Cole.

"I don't care; it's a silly game anyway," I frown.

"I expect better behavior from you, young lady," Mom scolds. "You want us to buy you an expensive cell phone, but you aren't mature enough to play a simple board game without getting upset. Now help put this game back together."

I feel like crying, but I sniff back the tears and set the pieces where they belong on the Monopoly board, and the play continues.

Dad exits the game soon after I do, when he has to pay Mom $1,400 for landing on Pennsylvania Avenue.

"You win some, you lose some," he says.

It's a fight to the finish between Mom and Cole, as they each add more and more houses and hotels to their properties.

Cole's stack of bills gets so high he has trouble counting it.

"Sophie, can you help me keep track of my money?" Cole asks.

"OK," I say, taking over management of the bank.

"Thanks for helping me out, Sis."

Cole picks the Chance card that makes him pay money for houses and hotels, and ends up broke. Mom is the champion.

"I guess Mom chose the car as her man because she's driving off with all the money," Cole jokes, and we all laugh.

We begin to put up the game pieces.

"Mom, Dad, Cole, I'm sorry I messed up the game earlier," I apologize.

"That's fine, Honey," says Mom, giving me a hug. "Just focus more on having fun than winning next time."

"I want to play Video Rangers when we have game night again." Cole says, getting up from the table.

"The point of family game night is for us to disconnect from our screens and spend time together," says Mom, "so individual video games will definitely not be allowed."

Cole and I go upstairs for our baths and get dressed for bed.

"I'm proud of how you handled yourself after the game, young lady," Dad says during tuck-in time that night. "Losing with grace is just as important as winning."

"Thanks Daddy," I say. "I really did want to win, but I had fun being with you, Mom and Cole, and I guess that's the most important thing."

"That's exactly right," he says, kissing me good night.

Chapter 10

The Free Throw

Wednesday morning at school, I get more good news. "Chloe has the flu," Mariama tells me. "Looks like it will be just us at our lunch table this afternoon."

"That's too bad," I say, silently breathing a sigh of relief.

I hate that Chloe doesn't feel well, but I'm grateful that I won't have to make up any more stories about my cell phone today. Mariama and the other kids seem to have forgotten about it, but I doubt Chloe will.

We join Toby, Lucas and Nathan Jones at lunch.

"Where's Chloe?" Toby asks.

"She's sick," I say. "Hopefully, she'll be back tomorrow."

The boys start talking about an NBA game they watched last night, and I join in the conversation.

"That buzzer beater James Harden shot at the end of the game was awesome, wasn't it?"

Mariama looks at me in surprise. "Since when did you start watching the Houston Rockets?"

"I never miss a game," I reply.

"It was a good one," Toby agrees.

"You said you hated the Rockets the last time I asked you about a game," Nathan pipes up.

"That was before they got their new players," I lie. "Come with me, Mariama. I need to take my tray to the counter before lunch is over."

"What's up with you, Sophie?" she whispers as we move to the front of the cafeteria. "You never liked basketball before."

"People change," I answer.

"Some people change a *lot* when boys are around," she replies.

"I don't know what you're talking about. I just like to watch the Rockets."

"Yeah right. Well… I guess I'll catch you later."

"OK, see you," I say.

This is getting more complicated by the minute. Coming up with all these stories is making me feel like Pinocchio.

Chloe still wasn't feeling well on Thursday or Friday, and as I expect, no one else questions me about my lack of a phone.

Saturday morning, I ask Mom to take me to Dad's office.

"I left a notebook I need for my science project in his desk," I say.

"I could get it for you on Monday," says Dad.

"Well, I'm not sure exactly where it is, or whether I left my blue or green folder," I fib, touching my nose to see if it's the same size. "The report is due on Monday, and I need it this weekend."

"I guess we could stop by after Cole's game," Dad says.

I forgot that Cole plays in the basketball youth league this weekend. Even though I don't like basketball that much, it's fun watching him play with his team. He looks so cute in his purple and yellow jersey and high-top basketball sneakers.

"Has anybody seen my lucky LeBron socks?" Cole asks, coming into the kitchen.

Oops! I forgot to get them out of my backpack.

"I think they are in the dirty clothes hamper," says Mom. "You need to make sure to put them in after each game so they will be in with the regular wash."

"But I had them in the hamper last Saturday!" Cole whines.

"Just put on another pair, and come on so we won't be late for the game," commands Dad.

We pull into the parking lot and make our way into the gym. As we move to the bleachers, I see a familiar face.

"Toby!"

"Hey Sophie," he says.

"You're not in a game, are you?"

"No, I'm here to watch my brother Michael play. He's on the Hornets."

That's the team Cole's is playing.

Toby and his parents take a seat near the edge of the bleachers.

"Who was that boy were you speaking to?" asks Dad as we join fans for Cole's team in the center of the stands.

"He's in my class at school," I reply.

"Look Sophie, there's your friend Chloe," Mom says, pointing near Toby's seat.

Oh no! I thought she was sick.

I feel queasy to my stomach as I watch Toby smile at my best friend, then offer to share a tub of popcorn with her. She nods her head and actually eats a handful. I wonder what she is doing here. I don't see her parents around anywhere, and I know they wouldn't drop her off by herself.

The game starts, and I can tell who Michael is right away. He's a shorter version of Toby, with black curly hair, minus the dimples.

"Your friend's little brother is pretty good," says Dad after Michael shoots a three-point shot.

"Yeah, this game is really close."

"This is the first time I've seen you actually watching the game and not reading a comic book," says Mom.

"I'm getting interested in basketball," I say, stealing a glance towards Toby's seat.

Chloe is giggling something to Toby, and I see her father coming from the concession stand to sit beside her.

At halftime, Cole's team is leading 25 to 23.

"It's still anybody's game," says Dad.

"Go Lakers!" I yell when Cole's team hits the floor again. They play for three minutes with both teams trading baskets. Soon, the score is tied.

With ten seconds to go, Cole dribbles the ball down the floor and tries a layup, but Michael pushes him.

"A foul!" yells Dad.

Cole's team lines up for him to make a free throw. He throws up the first one and it rolls two times around the basket before falling to the side.

"Oh no!" says Mom. She closes her eyes as Cole takes his second shot.

Swish!

It makes it in and the crowd goes wild. The Hornets throw the ball in to Michael, and he races down the court to throw up the ball, which bounces off the rim.

Cole's team has won the game.

"Hey Sophie, Cole is a great player," says Chloe as we make our way out. "I've never seen him play in a game. Did you bring your new phone? What color is it? I need to get your number before I get home."

"What are you doing here?" I ask, changing the subject. "I thought you were sick."

"It was a 24-hour flu," she replies. "I felt better Friday, but the doctor said I had to stay home from school because I might still be contagious. My cousin Jaimie is on the Hornets team, and my aunt and uncle invited us to watch him. I didn't know that Toby's brother was on the same team, too."

"Great game." Toby came to join us. "Tell your brother congratulations."

"Come on, Sophie. We need to head to the office," calls Dad.

"Wait, what about your number?" says Chloe.

"Gotta go! See you guys on Monday," I say, rushing to the door.

Chapter 11

Office Antics

"Can we get some Sonic before we go?" whines Cole after we all pile into the car.

"Sure Champ," says Dad. "I'm sure you're thirsty after all that running you did in the game.

"What flavor slush do you want?" Dad asks as we pull into the ordering area of the drive-in restaurant.

"PowerAde, with rainbow candy," Cole answers.

I ask for a small grape slush, and Mom orders a chocolate milkshake.

I'm getting more and more nervous as I think about how I'm going to get Dad's phone out of the office without being caught. I'm glad I thought to bring my red messenger bag to slide it in. I also brought a couple of folders with actual science class notes in them in case anyone asks to see them.

We drink our slushes and shakes in the Sonic parking lot, and Dad and Cole go over highlights of the game.

"That little boy, Michael, gave you a run for your money, didn't he? But you all were able to pull it off."

"The coach had us using our zone defense after he saw how fast they were," answers Cole.

After we finish, we drive downtown to Dad's office.

"I need to get some of my files to bring home, so I will go in with Sophie," says Dad.

"OK," Mom answers. "Cole and I can just wait here in the car."

I grab my bag and follow Daddy into the building.

"I hope the janitors didn't do anything with my notes," I say.

"If you left them around the desk area they should still be there," says Dad. "They never throw any papers away unless I request it."

Dad has a separate office in the back of his dental practice, where he has a desk and keeps special files and papers. Cole and I like to sit in his office swivel chair and spin when we are there, so it's no surprise to him that my notebook might have been left.

When he turns his back to go through the file cabinets, I quickly open up the top desk drawer. No sign of a phone. I pull open the next two at the same time, but see nothing there, either.

Finally, I tug at the last drawer and it is locked. *That must be where the phone is!*

"Any luck finding your folders?" Dad comes to look over my shoulders.

"No, I don't see them here," I answer in a panic. *How am I going to get that drawer open? And why didn't Cole tell me I needed a key?*

"I need to use the bathroom, Dad," I say. "Can I keep looking when I get back? I know my folder's here, because this is the last place I had it. Cole was with me when I lost it, so maybe he knows where it is."

"OK, but hurry up, Sweetie. Your mother and Cole may be getting hot out in the car."

I walk toward the office bathroom and glance around to see if I spot a key anywhere. Nothing. I will have to get Cole in here to see if he can help me out.

I stay in the bathroom a few minutes, flush the toilet, run some water and come out.

"Can I have Cole come in to help me?" I ask my dad. "I'm sure he will remember where I put my notebook."

"You are usually so responsible with your work, Sophie. I'm surprised you left something here that was due on Monday," says Dad.

"I know, and I'm really sorry for losing it. I thought I had it in my backpack, but remembered I left it here," I say.

"I'll just finish up something on the computer while you and your brother search," he says.

I run out to the car to get Cole.

"I need you in the office!" I say.

He sucks down the last of his slush and sticks out his blue-tinted tongue.

Mom looks up from a book she's reading. "What's going on? Did you get your folder?"

"I couldn't remember where it was exactly, but Cole was with me when I left it, so I thought he could help while Dad prints out something on his computer."

"I need you to show me which drawer the phone was in," I whisper to Cole as we race back to the office.

"It was in the top one, by the eating area in the back," he says.

I hadn't thought to look there.

We speed walk to the kitchen area and I fling open the drawer. It's empty!

Chapter 12

Back to the Drawing Board

"Where's the phone!?" I hiss.

"I don't know," Cole shrugs. "This is where I saw it last time."

"Any luck with your folder?" calls Dad.

"Found it!" I shout, and pull one of the folders I brought out of the bag.

"Great, let's head on home," he says.

"What are you going to do now?" asks Cole.

"I'm not sure," I say. "I've got to come up with something."

"It's a good thing we went by the office," says Dad once we're back in the car, "because I still haven't replaced my phone that was damaged in the flood, and I forgot that I needed to go through those files for some procedures Monday morning. It's tough keeping up with my calendar without it."

"I don't know how you've gotten along with just a flip phone for two weeks," says Mom.

"I know. I don't know how I've done it either," Dad replies. "I guess I should head over to the Apple store after I drop you guys home."

When we get home, Mom makes us some sandwiches and sends us outside.

"You kids spend too much time on video games and the computer," she says. "It's such a beautiful day. Why don't you enjoy the sunshine for a change?"

I grab some water bottles, fruit and cookies to add to our lunch, and follow my brother out the side door.

"I'm sorry the phone was gone, Sophie," says Cole once we're alone.

"It's not your fault, Cole. Someone must have moved it."

"It can't be Dad, or he wouldn't be going to buy a new phone."

"I know, it must be in that office somewhere."

While we are busy talking, our friend Jake rides up on his scooter. I quickly gobble down my sandwich. Though he is the littlest kid in our neighborhood, Jake has an enormous appetite. It's like he has the scent of a bloodhound or something, because anytime we're out eating, he comes around.

"Hey Cole, what's up?" he asks. "How'd your game go this morning."

"We won, as usual," brags Cole, grabbing a basketball to dribble. Jake hops off his scooter, then snags the ball and passes it off to me. I try to shoot the ball and miss.

"You owe me a cookie for missing," says Jake.

"I didn't even know we were playing," I protest.

"Pay up." Jake puts his hand out.

"I'm giving you the cookie because I want to, not because I owe you anything," I say, handing over a Thin Mint.

"Yum, thanks."

Jake's in the second grade like Cole, but goes to the public school in our neighborhood, so they've never been in the same class. He has an older brother, named Marshall, who is in high school.

I sit and watch as the boys play basketball in our driveway court.

"Got anymore cookies, Sophie?" Jake asks.

I hand him over the last one. "Here, take an apple, too," I laugh.

I hear music ringing.

Jake pulls his cell phone out of his pocket. "My mom's calling to see where I am," he says. "I need to get home."

"When did you get that iPhone?" I ask.

"He's had it for a while," says Cole. "You probably haven't noticed, because he doesn't get it out a lot when we're playing outside."

This is the answer to my prayers!

"Can I borrow your phone, Jake? Just until Tuesday?"

"I don't know. My parents would be mad if I lost my phone," he says.

"I won't lose it," I promise. "I just need to use it for an important project at school. I will make sure you get it back by Tuesday at 4:00 p.m. sharp."

He looks at me doubtfully.

"Pretty please? I'll make sure my mom buys those strawberry popsicles you love for the next time you come over. Your parents won't know it is gone."

"Well... I guess it will be OK if you have it back by Tuesday."

"It's a deal then," I say, slapping him on the back. "We'll see you back Tuesday, and I promise I'll have the phone ready for you."

"And the popsicles," Jake reminds me before hopping on his scooter.

"Won't your friends ask where the phone is after you give it back to Jake on Tuesday?" asks Cole.

"By then, Mom and Dad will probably have my birthday phone here," I say, "or the one you saw at the office will turn up."

Or I will need to stay home for a sick day like Chloe. Making up all these stories is wearing me out.

Chapter 13

Show and Tell

I'm ready for school bright and early Monday morning. I'm happy I can finally show off my "new" phone to my friends, and hopefully get Chloe off my back.

"Hey Sophie!" Chloe, Mariama and Toby are hanging out by my locker.

"It's good to see you back at school, Chloe," I say, setting my backpack down and turning my combination lock.

"Yeah, I'm happy to be here," she responds. "Since I was feeling better on Friday, my mom was giving me more work to do at home than I have in class."

"Well, you haven't missed anything exciting around here," I say.

"The most interesting thing that happened was Nathan Jones made a basket in P.E.," laughs Toby. "He usually throws up air balls. Speaking of which,

I'm going to the gym to see if any of the fellas want to shoot some hoops before class."

"See you, Toby," Chloe says as he bounces towards the gym.

"You and Toby seem to be getting along pretty well lately," I say. "I thought he was *Icky*."

"On the field trip I realized he is actually kind of nice," she replies. "We talked a lot in the kayak and he told me about his family. His said his brother Michael has dyslexia, like me, so he understands what I go through."

Things are definitely not going the way I'd planned.

"I finally was able to get my phone set up," I say, pulling Jake's iPhone out of my bag. "So, let me put in your numbers before I forget."

"Cool!" says Chloe. "I'm glad you were able to bring it. I'm surprised you got a case with a soccer ball on it, though. I thought you wanted that pink and green one with the flowers."

"Yeah, well, my dad picked it out," I explain. "My parents don't know I brought it to school, so I'll just put your numbers in my contact list and put it away."

"Good idea. We're not allowed to have our phones out during class time, anyway," Mariama agrees.

After I type in the phone numbers, I press the off button. I hope this will buy me some time until I get my own phone.

I make it to my first-period science class just before the bell rings. A strong smell like sour pickles makes me step back.

"What is that odor?" I ask, holding my nose.

"It's formaldehyde," says Vivian Green, a girl who sits beside me. "We are dissecting frogs today, and it's a chemical they keep them in."

"Ewww, yuck!" I exclaim.

With all the excitement about Toby and my phone, I had totally forgotten that we were cutting up frogs as part of our life science unit. I guess it's good I was distracted, because I have been dreading this all term.

"Students, write your name on a slip of paper and place it in the pail I'm passing around," instructs Mr. Gilbert, the science teacher. After we are done, he pulls the papers out two at a time.

"Vivian Green and Mariama Asante, you will be at Lab Station 1. Cameron Hardaway and Nathan Jones, take Lab Station 2. Sophie Washington and Toby Johnson, Lab Station 3."

I can't believe my good luck! Toby and I will be partners for a few days, since we have to do the dissection and a write-up. I hope he's good at science, though, because I am squeamish when it comes to the idea of looking at a dead frog.

"Hey Partner," he says, joining me at the lab station. "Excited about our assignment?"

"I'm not looking forward to dissecting a frog," I say, "but I'm good at writing, so I can do a lot of work on our write-up."

"Just leave the slicing and dicing to me, partner," Toby jokes. "I think it will be fun."

"I expect all students to take part in each area of the assignment," instructs Mr. Gilbert. "Your grade will reflect your amount of participation."

There goes my idea of letting Toby do all the work with the frog.

We put on rubber gloves to keep our hands clean, then get our frog out of packaging that is on the lab table. Our frog is curled up, so I'm not sure how we will lay it on its back.

"Sometimes the solution makes the frog's body stiff," says the teacher as he walks by our area. "Massage it gently to lay it flat."

I timidly touch the frog into position.

"Let's name him," suggests Toby. "How about Freddy?"

Next, we have to determine if Freddy is a girl or a boy frog. This isn't as embarrassing as I think, because Mr. Gilbert shows us we can tell by looking at its thumb size. A fat one means he's a boy frog. Ours is a girl.

We cut off the hinge that holds Freddy's mouth shut, then examine its tongue.

It looks too close to a human tongue for my comfort. "Brushing my teeth will never be the same again," I tell Toby.

I fill out the note sheet that Mr. Gilbert gives us as we go along, labeling all the frog's body parts. This really isn't as bad as I thought it would be. It's kind of interesting seeing and touching the actual body parts we have been learning about in our science book. I kind of feel bad for all the frogs that had to lose their lives for our classwork, though.

"Good job, kids," Mr. Gilbert says once we've finished the dissection. "Let's clean up our stations."

All the kids participated except Vivian Green, whose face turned purple when we pulled out the frog's liver and had to be excused to the nurse's office. Poor Mariama had to finish everything up herself.

"We will spend class time tomorrow completing our write-ups," says Mr. Gilbert.

Toby took what was left of Freddy's body to the trash can for disposal. I see Nathan giving him the evil eye as he makes his way back to our lab table. Toby bumps Nathan's shoulder.

I thought things had smoothed out between them after we got back from Austin, but I guess not.

Chapter 14

Group Chat

I join the group chat at lunchtime. I've been missing out on a lot of information, not having a cell phone.

[Meet-up at the mall next weekend, 3-5] Chloe

[Count me in!] Toby

[Sounds like fun. C u there!] Mariama

Would I have been told about this if I didn't have a phone? How many other places have they gone without me?

[Special notes for science write-up on Quizlet] Cameron

[Thanks!] Chloe

[The Class of 2023 Rules!] Josiah

Rrrriiing!!!

I'm startled by the bell and scramble up for fifth period. I've barely finished my food for scrolling through old messages. It's like I've entered a whole new world.

[OMG, science is so boring] Janice

[U r so rt] Jackson

Buzz, buzz, buzz…

The phone vibrates in my backpack every few minutes, but I can't look at it in class. Mrs. Laurel drones on about the Battle of the Alamo.

I wonder what my friends are saying?

I slide my hand in my backpack to pull the phone out. It won't hurt to sneak a peek, will it? I glance down at the screen.

"Sophie Washington, what is that in your hand?" Mrs. Laurel asks.

"Nothing," I say, trying to shove the phone back in my bag.

"Put your hands up," she demands, quickly moving to my desk.

I blush as I hold the phone in the air.

"I'll take that, young lady," she grabs Jake's phone. "The school policy is no phones in class. You'll get it back when your parents sign it out from the front office and pay a $30 fine."

I put my hands over my face. What am I going to do now? Nathan glances over at me in sympathy when I look up. I sit through the rest of the class in a daze. Things seem to be getting worse and worse.

Oh, what a tangled web we weave when first we practice to deceive.

I think about a quote my mother once read me about lying. Since I first made up my story about having a phone, things have gotten more and more complicated. I have no idea how I'm going to get out of this mess. At least I won't see Jake until tomorrow afternoon.

"That's too bad about your phone, Sophie," Nathan catches up with me after class.

"My parents are going to kill me when they find out," I groan.

"Maybe you could offer to pay the fine from your allowance, or do extra chores," Nathan suggests. "Your mom picks you up after school every day, so at least she won't have to make a special trip to get it for you."

"That's not the half of it," I struggle to sniff back tears.

"What's wrong, Sophie?" Chloe meets us in the hallway.

"Mrs. Laurel took her new phone," Nathan answers for me.

"I need to go to the restroom," I stammer out before I start bawling in the hallway.

"Want me to come with?" Chloe offers.

"No, that's OK." I rush off, leaving my friends behind.

I tell my P.E. teacher I'm not feeling well, and spend the last two class periods of the day in the nurse's office. It's too late in the day for the school to call Mom for early pickup, so I rush out as fast as I can when the final bell rings. I do not want to answer any questions about this from my friends.

Chapter 15

The Dark Side

At pickup, I tell Mom my head hurts, and stay in my room doing homework until dinnertime. Cole bounds in around 5:30 p.m. holding a light saber and wearing a white robe.

"Why have you been hiding around up here all afternoon?" he asks.

"I'm scared to come out and see you," I reply.

"Fear is the path to the dark side," he says in a fake Yoda voice, swinging his light saber to and fro.

"Get out of here, Silly," I laugh.

I follow Cole downstairs for dinner, wondering what my next steps will be.

Dad and Mom are already making their plates when we enter the eating area.

"How are you feeling, Sweetie?" asks Mom. "Headache any better?"

"I think I'll feel better once I eat," I say. My stomach grumbles as I smell spaghetti and meat sauce. I'd missed most of lunch fooling around with Jake's phone, and I'm starved.

"Your birthday is on Saturday," reminds Dad, "so I hope you won't be sick then."

We bow our heads to say grace, then I slurp down noodles.

"You weren't kidding when you said you were hungry," Mom remarks.

Cole tells us about a fun project they did in his science class. "We mixed salt, milk, cream, sugar, vanilla and ice in a plastic zip bag, and it turned into ice cream," he describes.

"What a fun way to learn about chemical reactions," says Dad.

"We did that in science in fourth grade," I say.

"We are probably more advanced than you all," Cole teases.

I pick up a roll as if to throw it at him.

"Looks like someone is cured," Mom grins.

I do feel much better as we laugh and share our days. Dad tells us a joke he got from one of his patients.

"What does the dentist of the year get? A little plaque."

"I've got one," says Mom. "Why did the deer need braces?"

"Why?" says Cole.

"He had buck teeth."

After we clean up the dinner dishes, we all sit in the den watching a movie. Cole still has on his Star Wars get-up, and my stomach sinks as I remember his earlier Yoda quote. Everything was so much better before I told all those lies about having a cell phone. I've gone to the dark side, and I've got to get out.

Chapter 16

Jake

Usually the school day drags on, but Tuesday moves like it is on speed dial. Seems like one second I'm standing at my locker, and the next Mom is clicking the garage door opener to bring us home.

"Do you need to go to the store or anything, Mom?" I ask, trying to think of a way to get us out of the house before 4:30 when Jake will arrive.

"No, Sophie, is there anything you need for school?"

"No," I answer, tried of telling lies.

I sit outside watching Cole play basketball while we wait for Jake to come over. Maybe I can come up with another way to stall him when he gets here. There's still a chance I could get a phone for my birthday. I could pretend the birthday phone got taken up in school, get my parents to sign Jake's phone out, and then get the phone back to him without him realizing what happened.

Rrrruff!

I snap out of my scheming by the sound of Dash, Jake's golden Labrador retriever barking, as he makes his way down the street. Dash isn't the only one with him. His older brother Marshall is at Jake's side.

"Wonder why Marshall's coming?" asks Cole. "Think he knows you borrowed Jake's phone?"

"I hope not," I mutter.

The boys make their way up the driveway and I consider bolting, but figure it's no use.

"Hi Jake," I say. "Want some of your favorite strawberry popsicles? We got a new box."

Marshall interrupts before Jake can answer.

"We came here to get my brother's cell phone."

"I was going to give it to him today," I say, stalling.

"Great, hand it over," Marshall replies.

"Uh, it's in the house. I need to go get it," I say.

"We'll be waiting." Marshall leans against Mom's car.

"Remember the popsicles," adds Jakes.

Rrruff! Dash sticks out his tongue.

Chapter 17

Caught

Sitting in my room, I debate what to do. Running out the front door isn't an option, because the boys will see me. If I tell them the truth, they'll get mad and tell Mom what's going on, which will get me in even more trouble. Maybe I can make a bargain with them that will buy me more time. I go back outside with the popsicle box.

"I'm so sorry, Jake," I say frantically, "but I left the phone in my locker. I can bring it to you tomorrow, I promise."

"But you promised to have my phone here today!" exclaims Jake.

"You thought you could take advantage of a little kid and no one would find out about it, Sophie, but I'm not having it," warns Marshall. "Either you get his phone now, or else."

"Where is his phone?" asks Cole. "I thought you kept it in your backpack?"

"I did, but I put it in my locker," I say.

Dash moves to the popsicles in my hand and starts whimpering.

"Is there anything the matter, kids?" Mom peeks her head out the garage door.

I look at Marshall and mouth, "No."

"Everything's fine, Mom," I say.

"Jake is just coming by to get a phone he left," Marshall interrupts.

"You left a phone here?" says Mom. "I haven't seen one lying around. I hope we didn't drive over it."

"It wasn't on the ground," says Marshall. "Sophie borrowed it."

"You borrowed Jake's phone?" Mom looks at me quizzically.

"Just for a couple of days," I say, holding my head down. "I left it in my locker."

"You know better than to take another child's cell phone, Sophie Washington!" Mom exclaims. "Do you know how expensive these are? I am so sorry, Marshall. We will drive right over to the school and get it, and Sophie will be returning it this evening."

"Thanks, Mrs. Washington," says Marshall. "Jake told me that he'd let your daughter borrow his cell phone in exchange for some popsicles this afternoon. I don't know if he realized he hadn't made a very fair trade."

"No indeed," Mom says, looking at me sternly. "Get in the car, young lady. We need to get to the school before it closes."

Chapter 18

Phone Home

"How could you do such a thing!?" Mom exclaims as we speed down the road toward Xavier. "Taking advantage of a boy three years younger than you!"

"I wasn't trying to take advantage of him, Mom," I cry. "I just wanted to use his phone for a few days."

"That's another reason why you don't need something expensive like that of your own," says Mom.

"But all my friends have cell phones," I beg. "And even Jake has one, and like you said, he's three years younger."

Mom rages on.

Cole reads his Video Rangers book and tunes the drama out.

When we pull up to the school parking lot, I spill the rest of the beans.

"Actually, the phone isn't in my locker," I stammer. "It's in the principal's office."

Tears stream down my cheeks as I explain the situation. Mom listens in silence.

"Well, let's see if we can catch the principal before the school closes," she replies.

We are in luck when we enter the office. Ms. Gogal, the principal's secretary, is packing up her desk. Mom says that we are there to retrieve the phone.

"Sure, Mrs. Washington. Just sign this form and pay the $30 fee," she says.

"Why didn't you tell me you lost the phone in class?" whispers Cole. "You are in big trouble."

We walk back to the car and I continue to hold my head down.

"I'll see you in your room in five minutes." Mom directs me to head upstairs after we arrive home.

I get in my bed and pull the covers over my head, crying. If only I could rewind the days and erase this nightmare. The light stings my eyes as Mom yanks the covers from my face.

"I was so angry and disappointed when we came home that I couldn't speak," she says. "You've been lying to your friends and family for days, maybe weeks. What has it gotten you?"

"Nothing," I answer.

"Dad and I were debating whether you were mature enough to have a cell phone or not, and this is our answer."

"But Mom, I just wanted to fit in with my friends," I plea. "Everyone has a cell phone but me."

"That's no reason to lie and trick your friends," Mom says gently. "Nothing good comes from being dishonest to others, and I hope you've learned your lesson."

"I'm sorry, Mamma," I cry.

"Well, I'm sorry, too," she says. "As a special surprise for your birthday, we bought you your own phone that we were going to give to you this Saturday, but now I think we need to wait on that."

"No, Mom! Please. I won't lie again. I promise!"

"Seems like you've been doing a lot of promising lately, young lady," she says, shaking her head, "but not a lot of honoring your word. Now get up from your bed and take this phone back to Jake."

I trudge over to Jake's house and knock on the door. Jake cracks the door open and I reach my hand out with his phone.

"I'm sorry, Jake," I mumble, not able to look him in the eye.

"What about my popsicles?" he asks.

"I'll make sure we have two boxes for you the next time you come over," I respond.

"Awesome!" he smiles. "Make sure they are strawberry."

He shuts the door and I turn to make my way home.

That wasn't as bad as I thought it would be. At least I didn't see his parents or his brother again.

Dad is at an overnight conference, so thankfully I won't have to face him tonight.

Chapter 19

Honor Assembly

The next day at school, our first two classes are cancelled because of a special honor's assembly for elementary and middle school students.

"Report cards came out last week and we want to honor students who went the extra mile," says Mr. Jenkins, our school principal. "Twenty students in our elementary grades and 30 middle schoolers made all A's this term, which is quite an accomplishment."

Chloe sinks lower in her chair. She works really hard in school, but has a hard time making the A-B honor roll because of her dyslexia.

Mr. Jenkins reads through names in first grade, and then makes it to the second graders. "Jasmine Aiken, Penelope Lee, Michael Johnson, Cole Washington."

We all clap and cheer.

"I'd like to give special recognition to Michael Johnson," Mr. Jenkins continues. "He joined our school mid-year, and already has more reading points in our accelerated reading program than any other elementary student."

Chloe looks at me in surprise. "I thought he had dyslexia," she whispers.

"Way to go, bro!" cheers Toby.

"We'd also like to give a special recognition to Chloe Hopkins, a sixth grader," adds Mr. Jenkins. "Each of her teachers gave her special mention for effort and class participation."

I turn and give my friend a big smile. She still doesn't look happy.

The assembly ends twenty minutes later. My hands are tired from clapping so much. I didn't get recognized for all A's because I'd gotten a B in Texas history, but I'm proud that Mariama and Nathan made it this time.

"Your brother doesn't really have dyslexia, does he?" Chloe confronts Toby as we head down the hall.

"He used to have it, but he grew out of it," he stammers.

"That's not something you grow out of, Bone-head," Chloe hisses. "You lied to make fun of me. You're nothing but a dishonest creep."

"I didn't want to make fun of you, Chloe, honest!" He shakes his head. "I just wanted to be your friend."

"Well, I never want to speak to you again!" She storms down the hall.

"Chloe, wait!" He rushes after her.

"What a jerk," says Nathan. "Always trying to put other people down so he can seem like a big shot. He'd get just what he deserves if Chloe pops him one."

I'm not happy Toby lied to Chloe, but I understand why he did it. I guess he and I have more in common than I thought. We've both been hiding how we really are to make someone like us.

Chapter 20

True Friends

As I expected, my father was angry when he found out what happened. "I'm very surprised at your behavior," he says. "Your mother and I have decided that you won't be getting a cell phone for this birthday, and you need to repay us the $30 fee we paid to get Jake's phone back from your piggy bank."

My eyes start to water and I look down at the floor.

"Maybe next year, when you are more mature, we'll talk about the phone again," Mom says.

"But what am I going to tell my friends!?" I wail. "They all think I have a cell phone."

"What about the truth?" asks Dad.

"They won't like me anymore."

"I doubt this will change how your real friends feel about you, Sophie," Mom strokes my back.

"You just don't understand!" I exclaim.

"Let's get everything cleared up, here and now." Mom hands me the home phone. "Why don't you call Chloe and explain the situation? She and Dad watch as I punch in Chloe's number with shaky fingers.

Please don't be home, I silently pray.

"Hopkin's residence," Chloe answers on the second ring.

"It's me, Sophie."

"Hey girl, what's up? Why aren't you calling me on your new phone, or answering any of my texts? I dialed the number you gave me and a little kid picked up."

"Well, there's something I need to tell you about my phone," I say hesitantly. "It's actually not mine."

"Huh?"

"I borrowed a phone from one of Cole's friends so you all would think I had one," I burst out. "I thought everyone would think I was lame because I don't have a cell phone."

"Why would I think you are lame, Sophie? You're one of my best friends! This sounds about as crazy as Toby saying his brother has dyslexia."

"I know, and I'm sorry I was so silly," I say. "I hope you won't be mad at me for lying. I guess I didn't want to be different from everyone else."

Chloe was quiet for a second.

"I can understand how you feel. Sometimes it's not fun standing out from the crowd."

"Maybe that's why Toby fibbed about his brother," I continue. "It seems like he really likes you, and since he's new, maybe he thought that would make you want to be his friend."

"You might have a point, Sophie Washington," said Chloe thoughtfully. "He texted me that he was sorry again, and I felt kind of bad for getting so angry with him. I *was* kind of hard on him. I thought he was making fun of me. Maybe I should call him and accept his apology."

We hang up the phone and I settle down. I'm relieved to not have to make up any more stories. Keeping so many secrets from my family and friends was tiring.

Chapter 21

Happy Birthday

Tweet, Tweet, Tweet.

I burrow my head under my blanket to drown out a sparrow's racket, but it's no use. He's been chirping for the past hour and the sun is shining bright. Might as well get up.

I slide my toes into my bunny slippers and sigh. One year ago on this day I couldn't wait to get out of bed, but now I've got the birthday blues.

"Happy Birthday, Sophie!" Cole greets me with a toothless grin as I enter the kitchen.

"You lost your other front tooth," I remark.

"Yeah, it came out last night," he answers. "And once again, the tooth fairy forgot me."

"She's running late," says Mom, heading to the fridge. "You'll probably get something tomorrow morning." She grabs the milk and playfully tugs my ponytail. "Happy Birthday to you, Little Miss."

I thought that she'd still be mad at me for not telling the truth, but I guess not.

"Happy Birthday, Princess." Dad comes and gives me a big hug.

"Thanks Dad."

"Since it's your special day, we're having your favorite breakfast," says Mom. "Omelets and French toast."

"Yummy!" I smile.

After breakfast, Mom and Dad take Cole and me to the zoo as a treat. Most of my friends think the zoo is babyish, but I love seeing all the animals and feeding the giraffes, and since Dad works so much at his dental practice, it's especially nice to have him there. We stay for almost three hours, then drive to Star Pizza for a late lunch.

"Hey, isn't that the boy from your class whose brother's team I beat?" says Cole, pointing to a booth behind ours. It's Toby!

He sees Cole pointing.

"Hi Sophie," he calls, giving me a big grin. His mother, father and brother are with him.

"Seems like we see you everywhere," I say smiling.

"Great minds think alike," replies his dad.

He shakes my father's hand. "I'm Leonard Johnson and this is my wife, Vera."

Mom and Dad introduce themselves. "We're here to celebrate our daughter Sophie's birthday," Mom shares.

"Happy Birthday, Sophie!" exclaims Toby.

We settle down to place our order, and laugh and joke about our time at the zoo. After we finish our pizza, our server brings out a cake with eleven candles.

"Want to join us in singing Happy Birthday to Sophie?" Mom asks the Johnsons.

"Certainly," says Toby's mom.

They sing and I blow out the candles. Our parents and brothers begin talking, and Toby pulls his chair beside mine.

"Thanks for putting in a good word for me with Chloe," he says. "She called and told me you stood up for me yesterday."

"I could tell you didn't mean to hurt her feelings," I reply.

"It's hard being the new kid sometimes," says Toby, "but I'm glad I've made so many nice friends here."

"Yeah, I know how much you like Chloe," I say, looking at my fingers.

"She's nice," he answers. "And you're pretty cool, too."

I lift my eyelids in surprise, and Toby shows his dimples.

"Thanks so much for helping us celebrate," Dad tells the Johnsons. "We should be heading home."

"The pleasure is ours," Mr. Johnson replies. "Hope you had a Happy Birthday, Sophie."

I smile all the way home. Toby Johnson thinks I'm cool! I didn't get the present I was expecting, but this has turned out to be one of the best birthdays ever.

Dear Reader:

Thank you for reading *Sophie Washington: Things You Didn't Know About Sophie*! I hope you liked it. If you enjoyed the book, I'd be grateful if you post a short review on Amazon. Your feedback really makes a difference and helps others learn about my books.

I appreciate your support!

Tonya Duncan Ellis

Books by
Tonya Duncan Ellis

For information on all Tonya Duncan Ellis books about Sophie and her friends

Check out the following pages!

You'll find:

* Blurbs about the other exciting books in the Sophie Washington series

* Information about Tonya Duncan Ellis

Sophie Washington: Queen of the Bee

Sign up for the spelling bee?

No way!

If there's one thing 10-year-old Texan Sophie Washington is good at, it's spelling. She's earned straight 100s on all her spelling tests to prove it. Her parents want her to compete in the Xavier Academy spelling bee, but Sophie wishes they would buzz off.

Her life in the Houston suburbs is full of adventures, and she doesn't want to slow down the action. Where else can you chase wild hogs out of your yard, ride a bucking sheep, or spy an eight-foot-long alligator during a bike ride through the neighborhood? Studying spelling words seems as fun as getting stung by a hornet, in comparison.

That's until her irritating classmate, Nathan Jones, challenges her. There's no way she can let Mr. Know-It-All win. Studying is hard when you have a pesky younger brother and a busy social calendar. Can Sophie ignore the distractions and become Queen of the Bee?

Sophie Washington: The Snitch

There's nothing worse than being a tattletale...

That's what 10-year-old Sophie Washington thinks until she runs into Lanie Mitchell, a new girl at school. Lanie pushes Sophie and her friends around at their lockers, and even takes their lunch money.

If they tell, they are scared the other kids in their class will call them snitches and won't be their friends. And when you're in the fifth grade, nothing seems worse than that.

Excitement at home keeps Sophie's mind off the trouble with Lanie.

She takes a fishing trip to the Gulf of Mexico with her parents and little brother, Cole, and discovers a mysterious creature in the attic above her room. For a while, Sophie is able to keep her parents from knowing what is going on at school. But Lanie's bullying goes too far, and a classmate gets seriously hurt. Sophie needs to make a decision. Should she stand up to the bully, or become a snitch?

Sophie Washington: Things You Didn't Know About Sophie

Oh, the tangled web we weave...

Sixth grader Sophie Washington thought she had life figured out when she was younger, but this school year, everything changed. She feels like an outsider because she's the only one in her class without a cell phone, and her crush, new kid Toby Johnson, has been calling her best friend Chloe. To fit in, Sophie changes who she is. Her plan to become popular works for a while, and she and Toby start to become friends.

In between the boy drama, Sophie takes a whirlwind class field trip to Austin, TX, where she visits the state museum, eats Tex-Mex food, and has a wild ride on a kayak. Back at home, Sophie fights off buzzards from her family's roof, dissects frogs in science class, and has fun at her little brother Cole's basketball tournament.

Things get more complicated when Sophie "borrows" a cell phone and gets caught. If her parents make her tell the truth, what will her friends think? Turns out Toby has also been hiding something, and Sophie discovers the best way to make true friends is to be yourself.

Sophie Washington:
The Gamer

40 Days Without Video Games? Oh No!

Sixth-grader Sophie Washington and her friends are back
with an interesting book about having fun with video
games while keeping balance. It's almost Easter, and
Sophie and her family get ready to start fasts for Lent
with their church, where they give up doing something
for 40 days that may not be good for them. Her parents
urge Sophie to stop tattling so much and encourage her
second-grade brother Cole to give up something he loves
most, playing video games. The kids agree to the
challenge, but how long can they keep it up? Soon after
Lent begins, Cole starts sneaking to play his video games.
Things start to get out of control when he loses a school
electronic tablet he checked out without his parents'
permission and comes to his sister for help. Should
Sophie break her promise and tattle on him?

Sophie Washington: Hurricane

#Sophie Strong

A hurricane's coming, and eleven-year-old Sophie Washington's typical middle school life in the Houston, Texas suburbs is about to make a major change. One day she's teasing her little brother, Cole, dodging classmate Nathan Jones' wayward science lab frog and complaining about "braggamuffin" cheerleader Valentina Martinez, and the next, she and her family are fleeing for their lives to avoid dangerous flood waters. Finding a place to stay isn't easy during the disaster, and the Washington's get some surprise visitors when they finally do locate shelter. To add to the trouble, three members of the Washington family go missing during the storm, and new friends lose their home. In the middle of it all, Sophie learns to be grateful for what she has and that she is stronger than she ever imagined.

Sophie Washington: Mission Costa Rica

Welcome to the Jungle

Sixth grader Sophie Washington, her good friends, Chloe and Valentina, and her parents and brother, Cole, are in for a week of adventure when her father signs them up for a Spring Break mission trip to Costa Rica. Sophie has dreams of lazing on the beach under palm trees, but these are squashed quicker than an underfoot banana once they arrive in the rain forest and are put to work, hauling buckets of water, painting and cooking. Near the hut they sleep in, the girls fight off wayward iguanas and howler monkeys, and nightly visits from a surprise "guest" make it hard for them to get much rest after their work is done.

A wrong turn in the jungle, midway through the week, makes Sophie wish she could leave South America and join another classmate who is doing a Spring Break vacation in Disney World.

In between the daily chores the family has fun times zip lining through the rain forest and taking an exciting river cruise in crocodile-filled waters. Sophie meets new friends during the mission week who show her a different side of life, and by the end of the trip, she starts to see Costa Rica as a home away from home.

About the Author

Tonya Duncan Ellis is the author of the Sophie Washington book series: *Queen of the Bee, The Snitch, Things You Didn't Know About Sophie, The Gamer, Hurricane* and *Mission: Costa Rica*. She also writes feature articles for family magazines. Born and raised in Louisville, KY, Tonya has lived in Indiana, South Carolina, Michigan, Ohio and Louisiana and spent time studying in Europe. She loves to travel and learn about new people and places. Tonya lives with her husband and three children in Houston, TX.